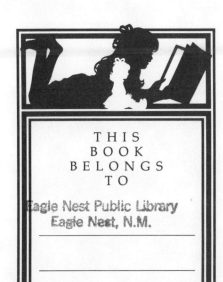

THIS
BOOK
BELONGS
TO

_____

_____

_____

DATE

Presents

The American Girls Collection

Kirsten
1854

Meet Kirsten · An American Girl

Kirsten Learns a Lesson · A School Story

Kirsten's Surprise · A Christmas Story

Samantha
1904

Meet Samantha · An American Girl

Samantha Learns a Lesson · A School Story

Samantha's Surprise · A Christmas Story

Molly
1944

Meet Molly · An American Girl

Molly Learns a Lesson · A School Story

Molly's Surprise · A Christmas Story

MEET
KIRSTEN
AN AMERICAN GIRL

BY JANET SHAW

ILLUSTRATIONS RENÉE GRAEF

VIGNETTES PAUL LACKNER

PLEASANT COMPANY

PICTURE CREDITS
The following individuals and organizations have generously given
permission to reprint illustrations contained in "Looking Back:"
pp. 54–55—The State Historical Society of Wisconsin; Emigrant Institute,
Växjo, Sweden; pp. 56–57 Courtesy Vesterheim, the Norwegian-American
Museum, Decorah, Iowa; Emigrant Institute, Växjo, Sweden; Emigrant
Institute, Växjo, Sweden; p. 58—The New-York Historical Society,
New York.

Edited by Jeanne Thieme
Designed by Myland McRevey

Library of Congress Cataloging-in-Publication Data

Shaw, Janet Beeler, 1937–
Meet Kirsten, an American girl.

(The American girls collection)
Summary: Nine-year-old Kirsten and her family experience many
hardships as they travel from Sweden to the Minnesota frontier in 1854.
[1. Emigration and immigration—Fiction.   2. Frontier and pioneer life—
Fiction.]
I. Graef, Renée, ill.   II. Title.   III. Series.
PZ7.S53423ME 1986   [Fic]   86-60466
ISBN 0-937295-00-0
ISBN 0-937295-01-9 (pbk.)

FOR MY MOTHER,
NADINA FOWLER

TABLE OF CONTENTS

KIRSTEN
A nine-year-old who moves with her family to a new home on America's frontier in 1854.

PAPA, LARS, MAMA, AND PETER
The Larsons sometimes long for Sweden, but they never lose heart for the challenges of pioneer life.

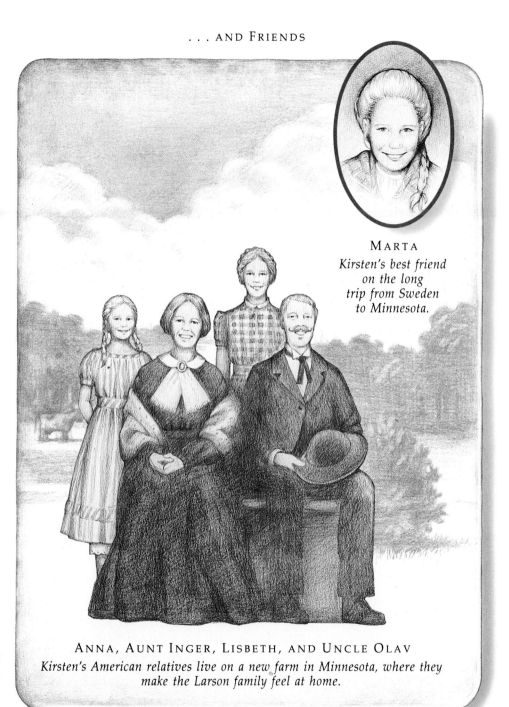

MARTA
*Kirsten's best friend
on the long
trip from Sweden
to Minnesota.*

ANNA, AUNT INGER, LISBETH, AND UNCLE OLAV
*Kirsten's American relatives live on a new farm in Minnesota, where they
make the Larson family feel at home.*

AMERICA!

"That's America!" Kirsten said happily. She stood at the ship's railing with her friend Marta and pointed to the green strip of land beyond the waves. Overhead, the tall sails creaked in the wind.

Marta shaded her eyes and pressed against the railing as though that would make the *Eagle* sail faster. "I can't wait to walk on land again," she said, and shivered.

Kirsten touched her friend's thin arm. "Are you cold?" she asked. "Let's go sit where the wind isn't so strong." She tucked her rag doll, Sari, into her shawl and walked to a coil of rope that was as high as a barrel. Then she hitched up her skirt and

1

climbed into a space just big enough for two girls to sit knee to knee and forehead to forehead. Marta crawled in after her.

It was warmer here in the coiled rope, but the wind still whistled overhead. Kirsten took her handkerchief from her pocket and made a cape for Sari. Marta's doll wore her apron like a shawl. "Soon we'll be on land again," Marta told her doll. "Don't worry about the wind."

Kirsten pulled a piece of hard, dry bread from her apron pocket and broke it in two. She and Marta fed their dolls before they chewed the bread themselves. "What's the very first thing you want to do in America?" Kirsten asked.

"I want to pick an apple," Marta said dreamily. "There are apples everywhere in America."

"Apples!" When Kirsten said the word she could almost taste the crisp, delicious fruit. "We'll pick cherries, too!" she said.

"And we'll get fresh bread," Marta added. "I think we'll be there by tonight, don't you?"

"Not if it storms again," Kirsten answered. She peered up at the darkening clouds and pulled her shawl more closely around her shoulders. Above

her head she saw the sailors crawling into the
rigging to adjust the sails. Then she heard Papa's
voice.

"Kirsten, where are you?" he called.

Kirsten stood and shouted, "Here I am, Papa!"
Strands of blonde hair pulled loose from her braids
and whipped across her cheeks when she raised her
head above the ropes.

Papa's black wool jacket flapped like a gull's
wings as he crossed the deck. "There's a storm
coming," Papa said. "It could be dangerous.
The coast is rocky here, and the wind is getting

stronger." Papa lifted Kirsten out of the coiled rope. Then he pulled Marta out, too. "Come below where we'll be safe," he said.

The clouds rolled like water boiling in Mama's black iron pot. The tops of the waves turned white and crashed over the sides of the ship. They dashed onto Kirsten's boots as she scrambled toward the opening into the hold. "Hurry!" Papa said. He held tightly to Kirsten's and Marta's hands.

As Kirsten climbed down the ladder into the hold, her spirits sank. Of course she didn't want to be washed overboard by the waves, but it was awful to stay in this small room below the deck. For more than two months, twenty Swedish families had been cramped together here. Each family shared one or two of the bunks that lined the walls, and everything they owned was stored in large trunks which stood at the ends of the bunks. The air smelled sour now, and it would be worse when people got seasick. No fresh air could come in when the sailors locked the trapdoor against the waves. And the hold was dark, even in the middle

4

of the afternoon. Just one oil lantern swung and sputtered over some tables in the middle of the room. Kirsten could barely see Mama, who was lying on her side in the narrow bunk she shared with Kirsten.

"Here you are," Mama said as Kirsten crawled up beside her. "I asked Papa to find you. I don't know where you can hide on such a small ship."

"Marta and I were playing. We could see land before the storm blew up," Kirsten said.

Mama sighed. "I prayed there would be no more storms so I could be strong when we land in America," she said. She had been sick since the first day they came aboard the ship, and storms made her feel worse.

"You'll be strong soon, I'm sure of it. Don't lose heart, Mama," said Kirsten. But now the wind howled like a pack of wolves. The waves beat against the ship's hull, next to Kirsten's head, and the ship tossed as though it might tip over.

Outside there was a loud crash. Mama put her arm over Kirsten's shoulder. "Don't fall off the bunk," she warned. Buckets tumbled over one another, and old Mr. Peterson's trunk skidded

5

*The waves beat against the ship's hull, next to Kirsten's head,
and the ship tossed as though it might tip over.*

across the wet floor. The lantern swung wildly, then
dropped beneath a table.

"Mama, Lars says the coast is full of rocks. Do
you think we'll be blown onto them?" Kirsten
asked. She could barely hear her own words above
the roar of the storm.

"Don't think about the rocks," Mama said.
"Let's think about Uncle Olav's letter instead. Do
you remember your Uncle Olav?"

Kirsten had heard about Uncle Olav so many
times she *thought* she remembered him. "Tell me,"
she said. She snuggled close to Mama and tried not
to think about the howling storm.

"Olav left Sweden six years ago, when you
were just three," Mama said. "He thought he could
make a better life in America. And last year, he
wrote to tell us about his new farm. The land is
rich and good there, and he needs our help."

"In Minne-sota," Kirsten said, stumbling over
the strange word.

"Yes, in Minnesota," Mama answered. "Now
you tell me something."

"Uncle Olav married Aunt Inger in America,"
Kirsten said. She thought this was the best part of

the story. "Aunt Inger came from Sweden, too."

"That's right," said Mama. "Olav said he married a widow with two daughters."

"My cousins, Anna and Lisbeth," Kirsten finished. "We'll be friends, don't you think?"

"Of course," said Mama. "We'll live on the same farm, and they'll be right next door."

The waves still pounded against the ship. In the dark hold, Kirsten hugged Sari's rag body and whispered, "We're almost there. We're almost home." She tried to imagine a farm right next door to her new cousins. She hoped this American home would be just like the one she left in Sweden, with the maple tree by the door.

When the storm finally passed, Kirsten felt like the barn cat she'd once fished out of the well. Her skirt and shawl were wet and stained. Her boots were soaked. But everyone was safe, the sky was clear, and the *Eagle* was sailing toward the green coast once more. Kirsten watched the seagulls swoop and dive as she stood on the deck with Mama and Papa.

"I smell the earth again," Papa's voice boomed. He held Peter, who was five, on his hip.

Mama smiled at the shore as though she greeted a friend. She leaned toward Papa, and Kirsten heard her whisper, "So many times I lost hope that we'd all make it to America."

"You're a brave woman," Papa answered. "You have heart. I'm proud of you and our children."

Kirsten's brother Lars, who was always talking with the sailors, pushed through the crowd just then. "The sailors say we'll land in New York tomorrow morning," Lars said.

"That's wonderful!" Mama replied. "We'll have fresh bread for breakfast, and I'll find a place to wash our clothes."

"They say we can't leave the ship until the health inspector lets us," Lars added.

"What's the health inspector?" Kirsten asked.

"He's a doctor who will look at everyone on the ship. No one who is sick can stay in America," Lars explained.

"But Mama's sick!" Peter cried. He held out his arms, and Mama hugged him.

"Mama has only been seasick," Papa said in his deep voice. "Almost everyone gets seasick on the ocean. The health inspector looks for illnesses like typhoid and cholera. Illnesses that kill people."

"No one on our ship has cholera," Lars said.

"That's right," Papa replied. "You see, Peter, we don't need to worry. Let's see you smile again. Tomorrow we'll be in New York, and then we'll start our journey to Minnesota."

When the *Eagle* finally docked in New York harbor and the health inspector said that they could leave the ship, Lars bounded down the gangplank. Peter scrambled right behind him. Mama and Papa went next, then Kirsten. She held Sari tightly.

Kirsten was bursting to run and turn circles on the grass she saw near the docks. She was surprised when she stepped off the gangplank and the ground seemed to spin around her. In Sweden, it had been steady under her feet. Here in America, it swayed and rolled like the ship she'd just left. She grabbed Papa's hand. "Why am I so dizzy?" she asked.

"We're all used to the rocking of the ship," Papa answered. "Now we have to get used to dry land all over again."

For a minute, Kirsten stood still. Then she turned and looked back at the *Eagle.* When they boarded the small ship, no one had known what to expect. There had been dangerous storms at sea. They had been sick. But at last they had arrived in America.

What will happen now? Kirsten wondered. But she was more curious than afraid. On wobbly legs, she followed Mama and Papa up the path into the park near the dock.

LOST

Kirsten sat under an oak tree with Mama and Peter. She patted down the grass to make a bed for Sari. Although it was only June, the grass here in the park was already as dry as straw. Summer was so hot in America! Three months ago, when they left the farm in Sweden, Kirsten had needed her wool skirt and shawl. Now her clothes were much too heavy. Even without her quilted petticoats she was hot.

Peter lay on his stomach, watching the road. He was on the lookout for Papa and Lars, who had gone to buy tickets for the rest of their journey. Papa promised that later he would take Peter and

12

Kirsten to buy bread and milk. Kirsten couldn't wait. She wanted to explore this new town, New York. But Mama wouldn't let her go by herself. Swedish children could easily get lost here in America, Mama warned.

While Papa was gone, Kirsten watched the New Yorkers stroll by. The women and girls wore flowered dresses with lots of ruffles. The men wore tight trousers and white jackets. Kirsten looked down at her own tattered clothes. The only fine thing she wore was the amber heart her grandmother had given her on the day they said good-bye. "Oh, Mama, I wish we could wear such pretty dresses," Kirsten said. "Only the people from the ships look like this."

"Our clothes are dry and clean. We don't need to be ashamed," Mama answered. Her cheeks were pink again, and now she smiled. "Besides, how could I milk a cow if I wore so many ruffles?"

Peter made a face. He hated to dress up, even for church. Then his frown turned into a grin and he jumped to his feet. "Here come Papa and Lars!" he called.

Lars held a handful of cherries. Papa scooped more fruit from the knapsack slung over his arm. He gave one big handful to Peter and another to Kirsten. Then he knelt beside Mama to share what was left.

"I've never seen such huge black cherries," Mama said.

"Everything in America is big!" Lars announced. "Wait until you see New York."

"And there will be more to see tomorrow," Papa added in a hearty voice. "I just bought our tickets for the trip west. We leave in the morning."

"Did you find an honest agent?" Mama asked with a worried frown. "Old Mr. Peterson was cheated of his money by a dishonest agent. I didn't know there were so many thieves in America."

Papa put his hand on her shoulder. "Yes, our agent is a good man. He left Sweden four years ago, and he knows English well. And he helped me change our money at a bank."

Mama still sighed. "It's such a long way to Minnesota," she said.

"But the agent will guide us all the way to the Mississippi River. He says we'll have to travel only a few weeks more," Papa replied. "And now that we're on land, we'll get our strength back quickly." He smiled. "Don't lose heart."

Mama smiled back. "No, I won't lose heart now."

Peter tugged the sleeve of Papa's shirt. "Let's go buy our milk and bread!" he said.

Mama handed Kirsten the milk pitcher. "Stay close to your father," she warned Kirsten and Peter. "Remember, you don't speak English yet."

 Papa took Peter's hand as they walked along the wide, crowded street called Broadway. Kirsten skipped beside them. She held the milk pitcher tightly in one arm and Sari in the other.

Kirsten had never seen so many horses, so many wagons, buggies, carts. Men and women filled the sidewalks. Children darted among them. In her small town in Sweden, Kirsten had known everyone she met. Here, everyone was a stranger. These Americans chattered, called, and shouted all around her. Kirsten couldn't understand a single word they said.

She walked with Papa past carts full of onions

and potatoes. Chickens and ducks fluttered and squawked in their coops as they waited to be sold. "Papa," Kirsten begged, "slow down! I want to look around."

Now there were candy stores, shops that sold tobacco, candles, tinware, cloth—oh, everything. "Here's the bread shop," Papa said. Round loaves of wheat bread were stacked inside the shop window. Papa carefully counted out two American coins, and the shopkeeper gave him several rolls. He handed one to Kirsten and one to Peter. "Now we'll get milk," he said.

The fresh bread was soft and sweet. Kirsten tried to eat slowly to make it last. She kept her eye on Papa's broad shoulders as she walked down the busy street, munching. She saw women holding huge baskets heaped with fruit. She couldn't understand what the women said, but the red berries in their baskets reminded her of the delicious cloudberries her grandmother gathered in Sweden.

Kirsten paused a moment by a gray-headed berry seller. Then a boy carrying a tray of silvery fish bumped her. She almost stumbled over a small black boy who polished a man's boots. "Wait, Papa!" she called over the racket of the horses' hooves on cobblestones.

But Papa was gone. Kirsten had lost sight of him in the crowd.

Clutching Sari, Kirsten ran. She squeezed between women with their shopping baskets. "Papa, wait for me!" she called. But she didn't see Papa. Lots of little boys chased through the crowd, but not one of them was Peter.

Maybe Papa and Peter are already at the milk shop, Kirsten thought. *Maybe they're waiting for me to come with the milk pitcher.* She hurried along, looking in each shop window for cheese and barrels of milk.

Where was the milk shop? Was it on the other side of the street? Kirsten climbed around pigs that poked their snouts in the trash of the gutter. Then she dodged in front of a buggy, ran across the street, and headed down the row of shops. She

"Papa!" Kirsten called.
Her cry was lost in the noisy street.

couldn't find the milk shop anywhere. And this side of the street was even more crowded with shoppers. The babble of their voices made her head swim. "Papa!" Kirsten called. Her cry was lost in the noisy street.

Kirsten tucked her necklace into her collar and hugged the milk pitcher tightly. Mama had said there were thieves in New York, a lot of thieves. They would steal anything. "Papa! Papa!" Kirsten shouted. Papa was nowhere to be found.

Maybe I should go back to the park, Kirsten said to herself. *Mama's waiting there.* But now Kirsten realized she didn't know where the park was, either. Which way had she come with Papa? How many corners had they turned?

She asked a woman with a baby in her arms, "Please, where is the park by the river?" The woman kept walking as though she hadn't even heard Kirsten.

"The park?" Kirsten asked a tall boy with black hair. He said something to his friend, and they laughed at her.

"Help me!" Kirsten cried out. "Please help me!" No one even glanced at her. Couldn't anyone in

19

this big crowd understand that she was lost?

Sun reflected off the cobblestones, and the smell of garbage made Kirsten dizzy. Her head spun as though she were seasick on the ship. But this time she wasn't seasick. She was frightened. What if she couldn't find Papa? What if she couldn't find the park and Mama? What would happen to her in this huge city if she couldn't find her family?

Again, she began to run. She stumbled and bumped into barrels. When a dog nipped at her ankles, she didn't stop running. Now she was on a different part of the street, where rough-looking men in bloody aprons sold wild game and meat. Gutted rabbits, squirrels, and deer hung from poles. Sides of pork dangled from sharp hooks. The buzz of flies hummed in her ears.

She headed back the other way, but she seemed to have turned onto a different street. The houses were all crowded together, and there were no shops at all. Papa would never look for her here! And every turn she took might lead her farther away from the park where Mama waited.

Kirsten wanted to be brave. She wanted to

have heart, like Mama. But she sank down on the steps of a brown house, hid her face in her doll's skirt, and wept. Tears ran between her fingers and dropped onto her lap. "Oh, Sari," she cried, "what if we can't find Mama and Papa? Will they go to Minnesota without us?"

After what seemed like a long time, Kirsten felt a touch on her shoulder. A brown-haired young woman in a long blue apron stood beside her. When the woman spoke, her voice was gentle. She seemed to want to know what was wrong.

"I'm lost!" Kirsten said. The woman didn't

understand. She looked puzzled and shook her head, and more tears ran down Kirsten's cheeks.

The woman spoke again. Now she made a motion as if she were pouring. Did she want the milk pitcher? Kirsten clutched it to her chest, and the woman went back inside the house.

"Sari, what will we do!" Kirsten sobbed.

Then the woman was back. This time she held out a tin cup of water. Gratefully, Kirsten drank until there wasn't a drop left. "*Tak!*" she said.

The woman smiled and sat down on the step. She understood "thank you." But how could Kirsten tell her about Papa and the milk shop, and the park near the ship where Mama was waiting? How could they understand each other if their words didn't match? Hopelessly, Kirsten traced the dust at her feet with her fingertip.

Then she had an idea. If she couldn't talk, maybe a picture could talk for her. Carefully,

Kirsten outlined the shape of the *Eagle* in the dust. Then she drew two big sails over the ship. She pulled at the corner of the woman's apron and pointed to her drawing.

The woman smiled when she saw the picture. Quickly, she locked her door, put the key in her apron pocket, and motioned for Kirsten to follow her. At the end of the street, they turned into a smaller lane. After a few more turns, they were beside the river, where the ships were docked.

Far ahead, Kirsten could see the tall oak trees of Battery Park. And there was the *Eagle,* tied to the dock. Kirsten ran. She saw the path leading into the park. And at the top of the path, she saw Mama and Papa!

"Mama! Papa! Here I am!" Kirsten shouted.

Mama turned and shaded her eyes to look. Papa began to run down the path, his boots scattering gravel. Kirsten flung herself first into Papa's arms, then into Mama's.

"Kirsten, you frightened us!" Papa said. "We couldn't find you anywhere!"

"I thought you would leave New York without me," Kirsten whispered against Mama's neck. Mama's shoulder smelled wonderfully of soap and dry grass. The sun made her hair look like gold.

"What?" Mama said. "We would never, never leave you! But how did you find your way back?"

Kirsten realized that the kind woman was gone. She pointed to her, walking away along the path beside the river. "I drew a picture of our ship and that American lady helped me find it."

Papa hugged Kirsten again. "You're a very smart girl," he told her. "Be smart enough to stay right beside me the next time. Promise?"

"I promise!" Kirsten said, and meant it with all her heart.

ACROSS THE
NEW LAND

The next day Kirsten and her family
started the long journey across the
country to Minnesota. Not even Papa
could guess how long the trip would take. "The
agent will help us find our way, and we'll see what
happens," he said.

At the top of the path into the park, Kirsten
met Marta. "We're leaving today," Kirsten said.
"Are you going, too?"

Marta shook her head. "Not until tomorrow,"
she replied.

"Oh, no! I was so sure we'd be traveling
together!" exclaimed Kirsten.

"Me, too," Marta answered softly. "Are you

going to take another ship now, Kirsten?"

"No, I think we're going to take a train,"
Kirsten said. "What do you think a train looks like,
Marta?"

"I don't know exactly. My father says it will
make a loud noise and a lot of smoke. We might be
afraid of trains," Marta said.

Kirsten grinned. "Noise won't hurt us!" she
said. "And Papa says a train is like many wagons
all traveling together. Maybe you'll get on our train
tomorrow. Wouldn't that be lucky?"

Marta caught her lower lip between her teeth.
"Or maybe we won't ever see each other again,"
she said.

Kirsten took her friend's hand. "But your family
is going to Minnesota, just like mine is. We're sure
to meet on the way. At least, I hope so," she added.

"I'll miss you, Kirsten," Marta murmured.

Kirsten looked down at her dusty boots. Saying
good-bye to the people she loved was the hardest
thing in the world to do. She didn't want Marta to
see the tears that stung her eyes. So she took a
deep breath before she said, "Marta, I'll tell you
what my grandmother said to me when we left

Sweden. Mormor said, 'When you're lonely, look at the sun. Remember that we all see the same sun.' "

"Do you do that?" Marta asked. "Do you look at the sun and think of your grandmother?"

"When I miss Mormor, I look at the sun and pray for her," Kirsten said.

Now Marta managed a small smile. "Then when I miss you, I'll look at the sun. Will you do the same?"

"Yes. And say a prayer. I will. I'll say, 'God bless Marta.' "

"I'll say a prayer, too," Marta agreed. "And I'll be looking for you everywhere."

Kirsten sighed. She was going to another new place. It seemed to her she would always feel like a Swedish girl who was far from home. Home—that's a place where you're happy, a place where you belong. *How can America ever really be my home?* she thought. Then she followed her parents down the path to meet the agent and ten new families.

First there was a fierce roar and a hiss, then the long scream of a whistle. Kirsten's heart flip-flopped. Maybe Marta was right to be afraid of trains. The engine looked like a black iron house on fire. Smoke boiled up from the giant smokestack. Live sparks and red coals showered down with the smoke. Kirsten stayed close to Mama. But Mama was worried, too. She squeezed Kirsten's hand extra hard as they climbed aboard.

Inside, the train was so hot it felt ready to explode. There was coal grit on the floor and cinders in the air. Kirsten could hardly get her breath. She saw that the windows had been nailed shut. The agent said the train would be safer this way.

Papa and Lars stood near the door. Kirsten was squeezed beside Mama and Peter on a bench under the windows. Trunks and bundles were piled up in front of them. Kirsten was used to being crowded, but now she felt as if she were packed up inside their big painted trunk.

"Aren't we there yet?" Peter complained.

"Hush, we haven't even started to move," Mama said.

Some of the old folks closed their eyes, and Kirsten knew they were praying that the train wouldn't catch on fire. Then it began to move. It bumped and lurched and screeched over the metal rails. Peter hid his face in Mama's lap. The men were quiet, and even Lars' eyes were wide. The train began to huff and chug. Through the small window, Kirsten saw houses and trees moving backwards. The huffing and chugging grew louder, and the trees went by very quickly. Lars called out, "We're going faster than a horse can run! Faster than the fastest horse can run!" Dizzy, Kirsten closed her eyes. The train groaned and swayed. Even though she couldn't see, she felt the speed with which it carried them west.

For days, the train traveled through fields and forests. When they stopped for water, a man from the railroad opened the door for a few minutes, but the air stayed hot and hard to breathe. Everyone was quiet, dazed by the heat. Now and then Mama opened the food trunk, but not even Lars was very hungry. When Kirsten caught his eye, he gave her a sad smile. She knew he hated to be trapped inside even more than she did.

CHICAGO

At last they reached Chicago. A hot strong
wind blew dirt up from the streets, but Kirsten
didn't care how dirty it was. Here she could walk
again, and run! Papa said that in a few days they
would join a big group of pioneers traveling to the
Mississippi River in wagons. But first they would
rest here, in a boarding house.

It was good to be in a house again, although
this boarding house reminded Kirsten of their big
barn in Sweden. The long, open sleeping room
upstairs was like the loft where Papa stored hay,
except it was filled with row after row of beds and
crowded with people's belongings. In the kitchen
there were big tubs for Mama to wash their clothes
in. When the laundry was finished, Mama sent
Kirsten and Peter out into the back yard to get
some sun. Kirsten found herself on a long porch
filled with children. She was used to smiling at
other girls, wishing she spoke their language so that
they could talk to each other. But now she heard

30

"You're here! You're here!"
Kirsten repeated over and over.

someone call her name: "Kirsten Larson!"

It was Marta! Her thick braid swinging, she
ran from between the rows of shirts and underwear
drying on the clotheslines. She grabbed Kirsten's
shoulders, Kirsten grabbed Marta's waist, and they
whirled and whirled.

"You're here! You're here!" Kirsten repeated
over and over.

"So are you!" Marta answered, again and again.

That evening, Marta's family sat down with
Kirsten's family for roast pork and potatoes. Marta's
father said, "We're back with our friends again.
We'll stay together now until we get to Minnesota."
Under the table Kirsten and Marta held hands.
Kirsten couldn't believe her good luck. At last
America was beginning to feel like home—with
good food, a real bed to sleep in, and best of all,
friends.

C H A P T E R
F O U R
———
A SAD
JOURNEY

Kirsten liked the Mississippi riverboat
the moment she saw it. It was white,
with a pair of wings painted in bright
red on the sides. The boat was named *The Redwing,*
like the red-winged blackbirds that called to one
another along the riverbank. *The Redwing* had
broad decks and a big paddle wheel.

Right away Kirsten wanted to run upstairs to
the wide upper deck. She grabbed Marta's hand,
ducked under a rope, and skipped up the steps. But
before they were to the top step a sailor stopped
them. They didn't understand his words, but they
knew his gesture meant "Get down!"

That evening as they ate their meal of dried

pork and bread, Kirsten asked Papa, "Why can't
we go up on the big deck? No one is out there."

"That deck is for rich people," Papa said.

"If we paid more money could we go up
there?" asked Kirsten.

Papa rubbed his forehead. "We only have a
little money left, Kirsten. And when we leave this
boat we'll still have to hire a wagon to reach Olav's
farm."

"You've managed our money well," Mama said
to Papa. To Kirsten she said crossly, "Don't ask for
so much!"

Kirsten was surprised. Mama never talked
harshly to her. Why was she cross now? Their long
trip was almost over. In a few days they would be
at Uncle Olav's.

Kirsten looked closely at her mother. "What's
wrong, Mama?" she asked.

Mama said softly, "I'm cross because I'm
worried. As we boarded the boat, the sailors were
burying a passenger who died of cholera."

"Don't worry so," Lars said to Mama. "We
won't get sick! Look at us. We're healthy."

Lars was right. They were strong from walking

beside the wagons on the way to the river and tan
from the prairie sun. But Mama didn't smile.
"Cholera kills strong ones just like weak ones," she
said. "Pray to God that we get safely to Uncle
Olav's."

For two days, Kirsten and Marta played
together on the riverboat. They watched the hawks
circling overhead and counted the fish that jumped
from the water. But the third morning, Marta
wasn't on the small deck where they were allowed
to walk. Marta's father was there alone. He stood at
the railing, staring straight ahead at the wide,
brown river.

"Where's Marta?" Kirsten asked him.

"Our Marta's very sick," he said. He gripped
the railing so tightly that his knuckles were white.
"With cholera."

Kirsten's head buzzed. Cholera! Last night after
supper, Marta had played with her right here on
deck. Last night Marta was perfectly fine. She
couldn't have cholera now.

"How can she be sick?" Kirsten asked. "She
was well yesterday."

"During the night she doubled up with a pain

in her belly. Now she aches and moans and burns with a fever. The captain made us take her to the sick bay," he said.

"Can I go see her?"

Marta's father took Kirsten's wrist firmly. "No, Kirsten. You mustn't. You could get sick, too. Marta's mother is with her. That's all we can do."

But Kirsten had to see Marta. She ran down below the decks, to the part of the boat called the sick bay. Marta was there, lying on a straw mat near the entrance. Her knees were drawn up to her chest. Her mouth was open as though she couldn't breathe. When her mother tried to wipe her forehead, Marta trembled and moaned. Her lips were dry and cracked and her eyelids fluttered.

"Marta," Kirsten whispered. She took a step toward her friend, but Marta's mother sent her away. "Go back to your family, Kirsten. It's dangerous for you here. Marta will get better, you'll see."

Still, Kirsten stayed near the sick bay until Mama found her. "I've looked everywhere for you!" Mama said. "There's nothing we can do for Marta. Not with cholera. You must take care of yourself,

Kirsten! Stay close to me and Papa, please."

So Kirsten stayed close to Mama, but her thoughts were with her sick friend. She told herself that Marta would get well. Over and over she said, *She must get well!*

Kirsten wasn't able to eat, and that night she was sure she would never sleep. But she fell into a restless doze. Later, she woke up with a start. Something was terribly wrong, but in her sleep she'd forgotten what it could be. Then she remembered Marta.

Kirsten ran down to the sick bay. Through the

parted curtains she saw that Marta was gone. *She's better then,* Kirsten thought. She ran up to the deck to find her friend.

The sun was just rising. The riverboat was anchored at a sandy beach below tall bluffs. A gangplank had been lowered for some sailors, who carried a wooden box on their shoulders. They walked along the shore.

Marta's father stood at the railing where Kirsten had seen him last. His arm was around Marta's mother.

Kirsten grabbed Marta's father's sleeve. "Where's Marta?" she asked.

He pointed to the sailors with their box. "Our Marta died last night, Kirsten. The sailors will bury her here. Her soul is in heaven." Then he hid his face in his hand.

"She can't be dead!" Kirsten cried. "She can't be!" Kirsten felt as though her heart was ripped in two. She heard deep sobs that hardly seemed her own. They filled up her chest. She tried to say her friend's name, but her lips wouldn't form the words.

Then Kirsten felt Mama's arms around her, and

Mama cradled her and said softly,
"Let her have her tears."

Papa patted her shoulder. "Enough crying. Stop now, Kirsten," he said.

But Mama cradled her and said softly, "Let her have her tears."

C H A P T E R
F I V E

—

HOME AT LAST

It was raining when the Larsons left *The Redwing*. Kirsten didn't watch the riverboat pull away from the dock. She didn't ever want to see that boat again, because Marta had died on it. She was lonely for Marta, and there wasn't any sun in Minnesota to look at with a prayer. So Kirsten looked at the town of Riverton. She saw wet houses, wet trees, and wet horses pulling wagons loaded with wet logs. She blinked into the rain. "God bless you, Marta," she whispered.

Mama touched her cheek. "Cheer up, Kirsten! When Papa and the boys come back with a wagon, it will only take a few hours to reach Olav's farm."

41

But Papa frowned with worry when he strode back to the dock where Kirsten and Mama waited. "We don't have enough money left to rent a horse and wagon," he said.

Mama's shoulders slumped. "What will we do?" she asked.

Papa made his voice strong. "We have our good legs. We'll walk to Olav's farm. We'll just have to leave the trunks here."

Mama looked first at the big painted trunk that held their most precious things, then at the black food trunk with Papa's name lettered on its side. "Everything we own in the world is in these trunks," she said sadly. "How can we get along without our clothes and your tools?"

"We'll take what we can carry now, and we'll have the trunks shipped later," Papa said. "Don't lose heart." He began taking blankets and tools from the big trunk.

After a moment, Mama said, "It can't be helped. We'll send for them soon. People are more important than things, and we're all together and well, thank God." She made a bundle of the bread and cheese that was left, then closed the food trunk.

Papa said, "We need everyone's hands today. Kirsten, you must put your doll here with the other things. You can get her again when the trunks are shipped to us."

Kirsten knew she couldn't say no to Papa. Gently, she put Sari on top of the sweaters and linens in the painted trunk. Before Papa closed the top, she kissed Sari's faded cheek. "You'll be with me soon," she whispered. Then Papa fastened the lock, and he and Lars dragged the trunks to the warehouse.

The family followed Papa down the road along

the river, past tiny houses built of split logs.
Everyone carried a bundle, and they walked for
hours. Kirsten's boots were heavy with mud. Her
wool skirt was soaked through to her petticoat.
Sometimes she heard a cow moo, but there were
long stretches of forest or prairie between farms.
Even Lars was tired now. He walked with his head
down, his long hair plastered to his neck by the rain.

By afternoon the rain stopped. The sky was a
smooth, blue bowl. Meadowlarks flew up from the
fields, and daisies and black-eyed Susans bloomed
beside the road. The Larsons were a long, long way
from town when they stopped to eat lunch.

"Olav wrote us the truth," Papa said. "The soil
here is good. We'll have a better life." Before they
walked on, Kirsten picked a daisy for Mama to
wear at her collar.

Now Papa asked the way at each farm they
passed. At last he said, "The next one is Olav's!"
In the distance, Kirsten could see a house, a large

barn, and a tiny cabin. Cows ambled
down the field toward the barn to be
milked. Smoke rose from the chimney
of the house.

44

Lars and Peter began to run, splashing through puddles. Lars shouted, "Hello!" and Peter cried, "We're here! We're here!"

A man with a smile like Papa's came from the barn. Two girls and a woman ran from the house. They waved and called out, "Hello! Hello! It's you! At last!"

Suddenly Kirsten was shy. She shrank back behind Mama. Then she heard her own name above the shouts and laughter. "Kirsten? You must be Kirsten!"

The taller girl, who had brown braids and gray eyes, took the heavy bundle from Kirsten's arms. "I'm Lisbeth! I've watched for you every single day."

The little girl with rosy cheeks crowded in. "I've watched, too! I'm Anna!"

Everyone was hugging. Aunt Inger tried to get all the children into her arms at the same time. Papa and Uncle Olav pounded each other's shoulders. Uncle Olav grabbed Lars, then lifted Peter off his feet. Mama cried. Aunt Inger cried. Then they started hugging all over again.

Uncle Olav said, "Come see the barn!"

"No you don't!" Aunt Inger said. Her smiling

*"Hello! Hello!
It's you! At last!"*

face was flushed and red. "First we'll have supper. They're tired and hungry, Olav! They've come halfway around the world to get here."

"And we walked all day long!" Peter added.

Aunt Inger hugged Peter again. Then she turned to Mama and Papa. "You can get settled in your cabin after supper," she said. "And *tomorrow* you men can look at the barn while we women talk. Now come in and eat!"

From the doorway, Kirsten saw fresh bread and butter, a big bowl of potatoes and onions, and a platter of fresh fish on Aunt Inger's long wooden table. Her mouth watered when she noticed a berry tart cooling on the back of the stove.

"Don't worry about a little mud," Aunt Inger said as they began taking off their boots. Then she saw that their clothes were wet, too. "But look how you're soaked through!" she added. "You'll catch cold. We'll find you all some dry things right now." She bustled to a painted trunk like the one Kirsten's family had left in Riverton. From the trunk she took men's brown trousers and white shirts, a blue cotton dress for Mama, and another one for Kirsten.

47

"This was Lisbeth's, but she's outgrown it. It will do for now," Aunt Inger said. "Go put it on and come right down for supper."

Kirsten followed Lisbeth and Anna up the ladder to their place in the loft. Anna gave her a piece of worn quilt to dry her wet arms and legs. "Tomorrow we'll show you our secret fort," she said. "Lisbeth and I play there with our dolls."

"We'll tell you all about it later," Lisbeth added as she handed Kirsten a petticoat. "But let's hurry now. We're hungry, and I bet you are, too."

The dress from Aunt Inger was patterned with little red flowers. Kirsten pulled the soft cotton over her head and Lisbeth did up the buttons. Now Kirsten was dressed just like her cousins. She followed them down the ladder into the cozy kitchen.

When Aunt Inger saw Kirsten, she laughed and pretended to be surprised. "Who's this new girl?" she asked. "Have I met her before?"

Mama took Kirsten's hand and turned her around for a good look. "Why, don't you recognize Kirsten Larson, my American daughter?"

The next morning, Kirsten woke up in her very own bed in a small log cabin on Uncle Olav's farm. The cabin was made of split logs. It had a bare plank floor, a small fireplace, and one tiny window. Through the window, Kirsten could see a maple tree. *I'm home,* she thought. *My cousins live right next door. We'll be friends.*

The morning sun was already hot and grasshoppers jumped in the long grass when Lisbeth and Anna led Kirsten down the path toward the stream. "You didn't tell your brothers about our fort, did you?" Anna asked. "Our fort is only for girls!"

Anna's cheerful, round face made Kirsten smile. "No, Anna, I didn't tell them about the fort. I can keep a secret, I promise," she said.

"Oh, good!" Anna carried her rag doll under her arm. The doll's smiling, painted face made Kirsten miss Sari all over again.

Lisbeth held up her hand for them to stop walking. "Is anyone coming?" she asked Anna.

Anna scampered back a few steps and looked down the path they followed through the woods.

"No one's coming. We're alone."

"Follow me, then," Lisbeth told
Kirsten. She lifted up a pine branch
and stepped off the trail into the woods. A carpet of
sweet-smelling pine needles covered the ground
under the trees.

"We go to our fort through the pines so we
won't leave footprints," Anna explained. "We don't
want anyone to know where we are."

"Here's the entrance," Lisbeth said. She went
down on her knees and crawled into a tunnel made
by sumac branches. Kirsten tucked up the skirt of
her new dress and crawled after her.

The tunnel ended under the green branches of
a wild cherry tree. Lisbeth sat back on her heels.
"Here's our fort, Kirsten."

Anna pulled off her sunbonnet and hung it
from a branch. "Do you like it here?" she asked.

Kirsten looked around. The overhanging
branches made a small, cool room under the tree.
She let out a long breath. "Oh, yes!"
she said.

"Here's where our dolls sleep,"
Lisbeth said. She laid her doll on a bed

50

made of sticks tied together at the
corners with braided grass. "Now, come
up to the loft. Hold tightly so you don't
fall." She grabbed the lowest limb of the tree and
pulled herself up into the branches. Kirsten gave
Anna a boost up, then climbed after her onto a
strong limb.

"Here's where we keep a lookout for boys,"
Anna said, swinging her legs. "Of course we've
never seen a boy in the woods, but with Lars and
Peter here, we might."

"If we see a boy, we'll get down low and stay
quiet," Lisbeth said. "That's one of our rules,
Kirsten. Do you promise to keep the rules?"

"I promise to keep all your rules," Kirsten said.
She looked out over the trees. When she left
Sweden she never imagined she was on her way
to a hiding place in a cherry tree.

"Since you live here now, you must have a
place in our fort just for your doll," Lisbeth said.

"Choose where!" Anna insisted.

Kirsten peered down through the
branches into the fort below. "There,"
Kirsten said, and she pointed to a

*"Since you live here now, you
must have a place in our fort," Lisbeth said.*

moss-covered spot. She scooted down the tree and patted the moss. It was soft and cool. Oh, Sari would like it here!

Anna climbed down, too. She got her doll and walked her across the fort to Sari's spot. "I'm coming to visit," she made her doll say. "Where is Sari?"

"Sari's still on her way," Kirsten answered. "But come visit me! *I'm* here!"

When Kirsten's family came to America, they fit all of their belongings into two big trunks. If your family decided to move to another country, could you do that? How would you know what to bring with you? What would you leave behind? One of your relatives probably had to make decisions like these, because there is a story like Kirsten's in nearly every American family. Most people who live in the United States today had relatives who were *immigrants*—people who left their home country and moved to America to start a new life. They may have settled here more than a hundred years ago, or they may have come more recently. Immigrants still come to the United States today.

Many of the early immigrants came from countries where farmland was poor. People were starving because they could not grow enough food. Like Kirsten and her family, they came to America because they wanted new land and a chance for a better life.

Immigrants who had already come to America wrote letters back home to their neighbors and relatives, telling them that life in America was good. "The land is rich," they wrote. "The grass is so thick that in one day we can cut enough to feed a cow for a whole winter." They encouraged others to join them on the frontier in places like Minnesota, where there was plenty of good land for anyone who was willing to work hard.

People who decided to go to America could bring only their most important things with them. They filled their big trunks with clothes, blankets, tools, and food for the trip. They also packed things that would remind them of the people they loved and the places they left behind. A woman like Mama might have made room for beautiful cloth that her mother had woven, or for a bowl that her father had carved, or for the wooden molds she always used to decorate butter or cheese. What do you think a girl like Kirsten might have squeezed in?

When their trunks were finally packed, a family had to travel to a port city and wait until a ship like the *Eagle* was ready to sail for America. These ships were filled with cargo like lumber and iron, so there was only a small space on them for people.

Immigrants traveled in a part of the ship called *steerage*. People in steerage were cramped and uncomfortable. The ceiling was so low that a man couldn't stand up straight. There were no windows for light or fresh air. There were no bathrooms, and it was hard to

get clean water for drinking or washing. Families slept on narrow wooden bunks that were covered with straw. Often two or more people shared a bunk that was smaller than your bed is.

Usually a mother cooked her family's meal on the ship's deck. At the beginning of the voyage, a family's food was fresh. But there were no refrigerators in

1854, so the food soon spoiled. Before the passengers reached land, even their salted meat was rotten and their bread was moldy. Still, they ate this food because it was all they had.

When Kirsten came to America, a very fast ship could sail across the ocean in six weeks. If the wind was bad, the trip would take much longer. Sometimes immigrants died in storms and shipwrecks on the way to America. And even with good weather, many passengers got seasick. Some of them got terrible diseases, such as cholera.

Once an immigrant family arrived safely in America, the dangers of the trip were not over. Most immigrants could not speak English, and they did not have anyone to help them buy fresh food or train tickets for their trip to the frontier. Sometimes thieves robbed or cheated the immigrants.

Immigrating to America in 1854 was certainly dangerous, but it was exciting, too. If Kirsten's family had stayed in Sweden, she would never have seen the ocean or even a town more than 20 miles from the place she was born. Because they became immigrants, she traveled halfway around the world. She saw machines she had never dreamed of, like trains and paddle-wheel boats. She saw busy cities like New York and Chicago. She saw long stretches of open prairie and miles of rich farmland. And at the end of her journey, she had a new home in a new land, with a life full of opportunity ahead of her.

THE AMERICAN GIRLS COLLECTION

There are nine books in The American Girls Collection. They're filled with the adventures that three lively American girls—Kirsten, Samantha, and Molly—lived long ago. You'll want to read all of these books to see how growing up as a girl in America has changed and how it has stayed the same.

But the books are only part of The American Girls Collection—only the beginning. There are lovable dolls—Kirsten, Samantha, and Molly dolls—that have beautiful clothes and lots of wonderful accessories to go with them. They make these stories of the past come alive today for American girls like you.

To learn about The American Girls Collection, fill out this postcard and mail it to Pleasant Company. We will send you a newsletter with more interesting things to read about Kirsten, Samantha and Molly, and a catalogue about all the books, dolls, dresses and other delights in The American Girls Collection.

MOLLY
SAMANTHA
KIRSTEN

I'm an American girl who loves to get mail. Please send me:

□ The **catalogue** of
The American Girls Collection

□ The **newsletter** of
The American Girls Collection
(available after January, 1987)

My name is

My address is

City   State   Zip

My Birthday is   My age is

I am in   grade.   Parent's Signature

The book this post-   □ a bookstore □ a library □ a friend/relative
card is in came from: □ the Pleasant Company Catalogue

If the postcard has already
been removed from this book,
and you would like the Pleasant
Company newsletter and catalogue, please send your name
and address to:

PLEASANT COMPANY
P.O. Box 460
Madison, WI 53791-9634

DEMCO